THE 9 CATS
Go to the Jungle

By Calum Johnston and Linda Johnston

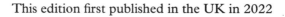

This edition first published in the UK in 2022

Text, cover and illustrations © Calum Johnston and Linda Johnston, 2022
www.cuddlecats-publishing.co.uk

Illustrations by Jacqueline Tee

A CIP record for this book is available from the British Library

Typesetting by Ten Thousand | Editing + Book Design
www.tenthousand.co.uk

ISBN: 9798849828817

Printed by Amazon

Once upon a time, there were nine cats, called Poppy, Molly, Daisy, Millie, Milo, Monty, Charlotte, Stella and Tiger.

It was a lovely warm day so Charlotte suggested going out into the garden.

Millie said, "Great idea – let's head outside."

Out they all went into the lovely warm weather. They could hear the birds singing and the bees buzzing.

Suddenly, Milo shouted,
"What's that over there?"

 Everyone looked and saw
where he was pointing and
saw a mound of dirt
with a hole in it.

Milo went over and jumped
into the hole and disappeared!
Everyone gasped.

 Tiger shouted,
"Where did he go?
Where is he?"

"I don't know," said everyone sadly.

Molly said, "We can't just
leave him like that."

And with that, she jumped in
the hole as well and disappeared.

Monty declared, "We have to go
in and help them, whatever's
happened, but we need one or
two of us to stay behind in
case we need help from here."

Poppy and Stella put their
paws up and said, "We'll stay!"

They felt more scared than
brave at this point.

"OK," said Monty, "stay near
this hole in case we need
to shout back for help."

And with that, they
all jumped
into the
hole.

Once they were all inside the
hole, they shrieked with
laughter as they went
down what
felt like
a big
slide!

When they
reached the
bottom, they
found themselves in
a big leafy green space.

As they sat there, dazed and
puzzled about what had
just happened, they heard,
"Thank goodness you're here."

They turned round
and saw Molly and Milo.

"We were so scared.
Where do you think
we are?" asked Milo.

Monty looked around and
listened to all the noises, and
said, "I think we're in a jungle!"

At that, he heard
I think we're in a jungle
being repeated in a
squawky voice.

Everyone spun around
and saw a large bird,
with beautiful colours
through its feathers,
looking back at them
from a tree branch.

Monty said, "That's a
parrot." He'd seen them on television
while he was learning about nature.

The parrot repeated his words
back and they all laughed.

The parrot looked at them and
asked, "What animal are you?"

They said, all together,
that they were cats.

Monty said, "We came down
a hole and just ended up here."

"Interesting," said the parrot.
"I'm just having some lunch here.
Would you like some nuts and fruit?"

Milo piped up, "That's
kind but no thank you.
Our food comes from a tin."

All the cats agreed with him.

Daisy said to everyone, "Do
you want to have a look around
this place now that we're here?"

Everyone agreed immediately.

Daisy turned to the parrot
and asked, "Will you come
with us please and help us
find our way around?"

"I would love to," said the
parrot. "How exciting,
having visitors with me."

So they all set off for a
walk in the jungle.

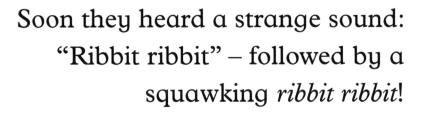

Soon they heard a strange sound:
"Ribbit ribbit" – followed by a
squawking *ribbit ribbit*!

Everyone looked round and
Molly said, "Parrot,
STOP COPYING! What
was that sound, do you know?"

The sound went again before
the parrot could answer, and
they all turned around and
saw a little slimy green animal.

Monty piped up, "It's a
frog! This is the first time
I've seen one for real!"

Parrot said, "These are my
new friends. They're an
animal called a cat, and
their names are Molly,
Daisy, Millie, Milo,
Monty, Charlotte and Tiger.

Frog looked at everyone and said, "You're all my friends too then. I'm having some lunch of worms and flies – would anyone like some?"

Parrot replied, "Thank you, Frog, but I'll stick with my nuts and fruit."

Tiger spoke up for all the cats and told him, "No thank you. Our food comes from a tin."

"No problem," said Frog. "You don't know what you're missing."

Charlotte piped up, "Who wants to move on even further now?"

Parrot and Frog thought that was a wonderful idea and all the cats agreed. Everyone started to move on again.

They walked on a little
further with their new
friends, Parrot and Frog.

Suddenly, Tiger gave a little
squeal and said he saw
leaves moving as if they were
walking along the ground.

The parrot copied what he
said, and everyone shouted,
"STOP COPYING, PARROT!"

Daisy piped up, "Tiger,
leaves can't walk – you're
just imagining it!"

They then heard a squeaky
voice say, "Leaves can't
walk, but we can!"

They all looked down to
the ground and saw these
tiny bugs everywhere.

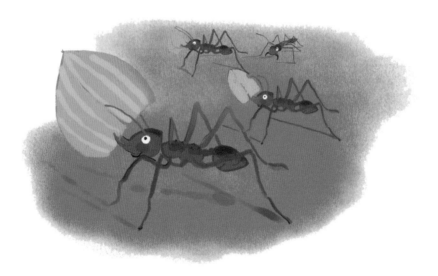

"These are ants," Monty told everyone.

"Yes," said the squeaky ant.
"We're carrying these leaves
to our house."

Parrot and Frog said, "These
are visitors, called cats."
They told them their names.

"I'm stopping for lunch soon,"
said the ant. "You're welcome
to share some of my bugs and leaves."

"No thank you," said Parrot.
"I like my nuts and my fruit."

Frog said, "I'm full up
from eating worms!"

Millie said, "We just
eat from a tin."

"Suit yourselves," said Ant.
"I must get back to my friends.
We work so hard, and as a team."

"That's a shame," said Tiger.
"We would love for you to
come with us for a little while."

They then heard another
squeaky sound and it was
the leader of the ant team.

"On you go, little one. We can
spare you for a little while.
Be back soon though."

"YIPPEE!" said the ant.
"I hardly ever get time off!"

And with that, they
all walked on.

As they were walking along,
they heard a little voice say,
"Hello, are you new here?
Never seen you before."

Everyone looked around and
saw a little green animal
resting on a large leaf. It
got up and walked along
the branch, turning
brown as it did so.

"This is my friend, Chameleon,"
said Parrot. "He can change
himself to many colours!"

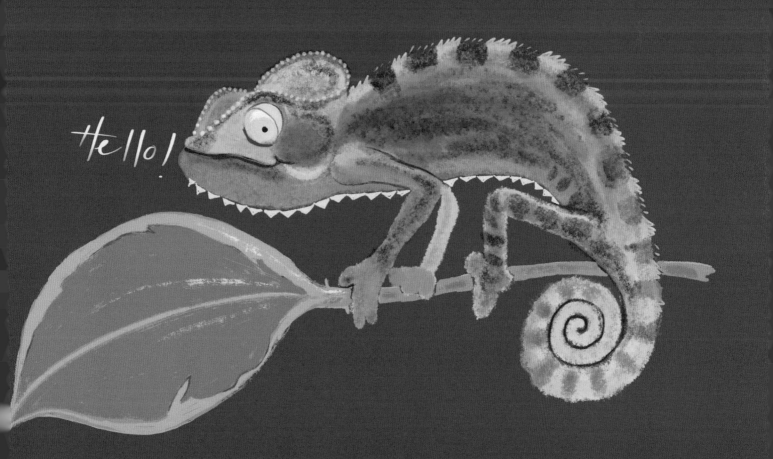

"Amazing!" exclaimed everyone
(apart from Monty because
he already knew).

 "It just comes naturally to
me," said Chameleon.

"These are my friends," said Parrot.
"They are an animal called a cat.
Their names are Molly, Daisy, Millie,
Milo, Monty, Charlotte and Tiger.

The Chameleon then said
that they were all his friends too.

"Would you like to stay for
lunch? I'm having yummy
locusts and grasshoppers."

"No thank you," said Parrot, "I'll stick with my nuts and fruit."

"I'm still full from my worms," said Frog.

"I'm full with leaves," said Ant.

"We only eat from a tin," said Milo.

 "OK, just thought I would ask," said Chameleon.

"We're showing our new friends, the cats, around the jungle," said Parrot. "Would you like to come with us?"

"I certainly would," said
Chameleon, and he changed
his colour to a happy pink.

And with that, they all set off again.

On they walked again, taking in the sights and sounds of the jungle. Parrot was copying some of the sounds of the jungle and getting on everyone's nerves a little bit.

Just ahead, they eventually saw a huge open space.

"I think something dangerous could live here," said Monty. "I saw on one of my television programmes that all sorts of wild animals could live in places like this. Maybe even huge gorillas."

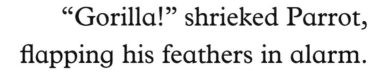 "Gorilla!" shrieked Parrot,
flapping his feathers in alarm.

"Calm down, Parrot," said
Monty. "I was only saying."

"No, really," said Parrot. "Look
quickly – it's heading towards us."

Tiger went and hid behind a
bush. Everyone scattered to
find a hiding place.

 Unfortunately, Millie wasn't fast
enough and got caught by the
huge animal. The gorilla
wondered aloud what this was
and if it might be a tasty snack.

Molly and Monty came out
of their hiding place and shouted,
"PUT HER DOWN RIGHT NOW!"

Parrot was flapping above
them and shouted loudly,
"LEAVE HER ALONE!"

The gorilla put Millie to his
mouth, but the next thing she
knew, she was catapulted
across the ground.

A passing bear had heard
all the commotion and
saw what was happening
and pounced on the gorilla,
pinning him to the ground.

Millie lay on the ground,
unable to open her eyes,
she was so scared. Daisy ran
over and pulled Millie to safety.

The bear held the gorilla
down and shouted, "Everyone
start running to safety!
I'll hold him down."

Ant said, "I'll stay here
and help Bear. I can
bite really hard."

Everyone started running fast
and shouted back to Bear
and Ant, "THANK YOU!
THANK YOU SO MUCH!"

When they felt safe, they
stopped to catch their breath.

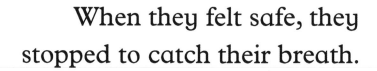

Frog and Chameleon
said, "It's been really nice
meeting you all. We're going
to go a different way."

They all said their goodbyes.

Parrot then said to the cats,
"Follow me – I'll lead you
to where I met you."

They all followed Parrot
and eventually came back
to the same spot and saw the
hole they had come from.

Parrot said, "You should go back into the hole and try to get home – you're safer there."

The cats all agreed and walked towards the hole.

Charlotte said, "It's been really nice meeting you, Parrot. We'll miss you."

"I'll miss you too," said Parrot.

The cats walked towards the hole and could hear noises from it. They could hear Poppy saying, "They're taking ages!"

Then they heard Stella's
voice saying, "Where are they?"

They looked into the hole and
were astonished to see that the
slope they slid down had
turned the other way and
they could slide back again.

They said a
final farewell
to Parrot
and got
back in the
hole and
slid back
to the
garden.

Poppy and Stella were so
happy to see them back,
and everyone hugged.
They looked at the hole
and gasped as it disappeared
before their eyes!

"What happened in
there?" asked Poppy.

There was the noise
of a tin being opened
in the house.

"Tell you over dinner,"
said Monty, and they all
bounded into the kitchen.

Poppy

Charlotte

Milo

Molly

Tiger

Daisy

Millie

Stella

Monty

Printed in Great Britain
by Amazon

10584322R00025